CALL ME CALVIN

Mary Vander Plas

illustrated by **André Ceolin**

ALBERT WHITMAN & COMPANY

CHICAGO, ILLINOIS

When Calvin was born, Dad said,
"Welcome to the world, Little Man."
The nickname stuck.

"Goodnight, Little Man."

"Great job, Little Man!"

For a while, Calvin liked his special nickname.
But now that he was growing up...

He was the opposite of tall.
He only felt little.

And not strong at all.

He couldn't even reach the freshly baked cookies on the counter.

In fact, he could barely see them. He could only smell them.

Somehow that made it worse.

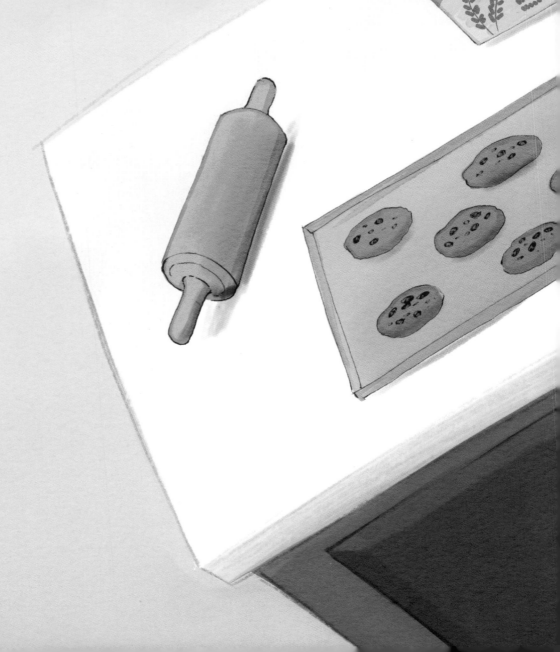

He was too small to climb the tree in his front yard.
The squirrels made it look easy.
They were small, too, but that didn't stop them.
It only stopped Calvin.

And no way, no how, could he make a basket.

He tried again and again, until his arms felt like noodles.

"Keep trying, Little Man," Dad said as he brought in the groceries.

Tired, frustrated, and even a bit angry,
Calvin squeezed his eyes shut.

Something BIG stirred in his imagination, until...

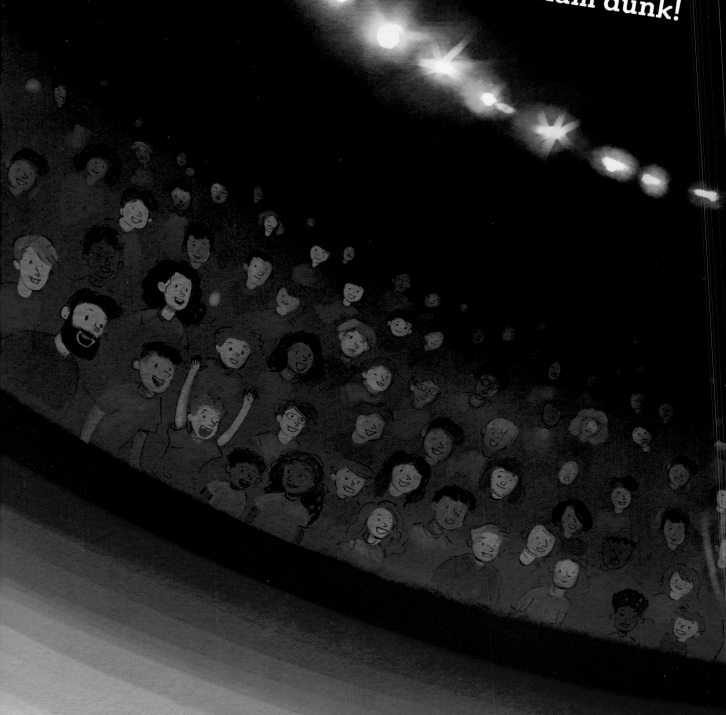

BOOM!

Slam dunk!

Then Calvin heard something he'd never heard when he was Dad's Little Man.

"You're as tall as a tree!"

Something even BIGGER stirred inside him...

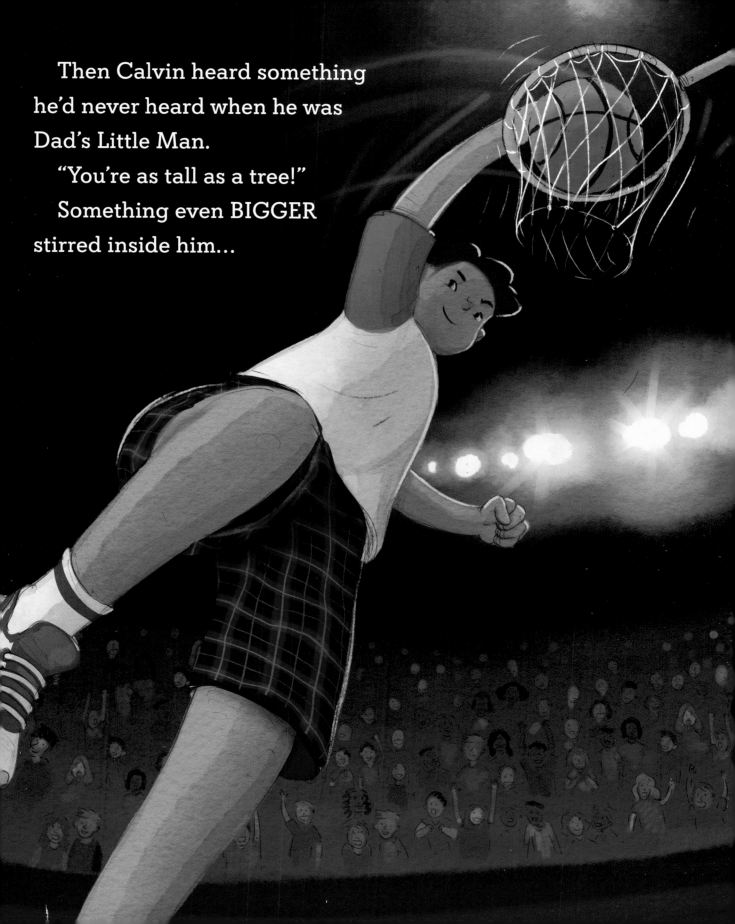

Calvin stretched toward the clouds, above all the other trees. He swayed and swung and danced until his leaves fell away.

Then Calvin heard a rumble from high above his limbs that sounded...

BIG...

LOUD...

STRONG!

Being the tallest tree wasn't enough. Calvin wanted to be strong, too, just like Dad.
His wide trunk shook.

Calvin rumbled and flashed and lit up the sky.

After, Calvin looked down
from high above.
   The tree branches were bare.
His hoop was knocked over.
He had scared the squirrels.

He'd even scared himself.

Calvin opened his eyes as the storm inside him settled. "Maybe being big can wait," he whispered.

"Hey Little Man, time to come in!" Dad
called. "Those clouds don't look good."
Calvin raced inside...

and jumped into Dad's arms. He fit perfectly.

"Instead of Little Man, can you call me Calvin?"
he asked. "I don't think I'm done being a kid."

"Of course, Calvin." Dad hugged him gently.

Calvin loved that Dad was big and strong. But he was also cuddly and comfy. And soft and safe.

Exactly the kind of grown-up Calvin wanted to be...

someday.

To my family, who is always inspiring me in big and small ways—MVP

To my son, and to all the children
with great futures ahead of them—AC

Library of Congress Cataloging-in-Publication data is on file with the publisher.
Text copyright © 2023 by Mary Vander Plas
Illustrations copyright © 2023 by Albert Whitman & Company
Illustrations by André Ceolin
First published in the United States of America in 2023 by Albert Whitman & Company
ISBN 978-0-8075-1044-5 (hardcover)
ISBN 978-0-8075-1045-2 (ebook)

Printed in China
10 9 8 7 6 5 4 3 2 1 WKT 26 25 24 23 22

Design by Rick DeMonico and Erin McMahon

For more information about Albert Whitman & Company,
visit our website at www.albertwhitman.com.